The Brocaded Slipper
And Other
Vietnamese Tales

The Brocaded Slipper
And Other
Vietnamese Tales

by Lynette Dyer Vuong
Illustrated by Vo-Dinh Mai

HarperTrophy

A Division of HarperCollins*Publishers*

First published by Addison-Wesley Publishing Company
THE BROCADED SLIPPER *and Other Vietnamese Tales*
Text copyright © 1982 by Lynette Dyer Vuong
Illustrations copyright © 1982 by Vo-Dinh Mai
For information address HarperCollins Children's Books,
a division of HarperCollins Publishers,
10 East 53rd Street, New York, NY 10022.

Library of Congress Cataloging-in-Publication Data
Vuong, Lynette Dyer, 1938–
    The brocaded slipper and other Vietnamese tales.
    Summary: A collection of five Vietnamese fairy tales,
including "Little Finger of the Watermelon Patch" and
"The Lampstand Princess."
    1. Fairy tales—Vietnam. [1. Fairy tales. 2. Folklore—
Vietnam] I. Vo-Dinh Mai, ill. II. Title.
[PZ8.V889Br 1985]   398.2'1'09597 [E]   84-40746
ISBN 0-201-08088-5
ISBN 0-397-32508-8 (lib. bdg.)
ISBN 0-06-440440-4 (pbk.)

First Harper Trophy edition, 1992.

A Scott Foresman Edition
ISBN 0-673-80140-3

To my father
who first turned my interest to other lands
and my husband
who turned it specifically to Vietnam

Table of Contents

Introduction

Fairy tales have always fascinated me, whether the familiar Grimms' or the more exotic ones from faraway places. So it was only natural that when I went to Vietnam and began to learn the language, my trips to the bookstore should lead me into a new world of folklore. And there, among the many new faces, to my surprise I found some old friends.

Here was Cinderella: Tam, to the Vietnamese. Like her Western counterpart, she was mistreated by a cruel stepmother and stepsister, then befriended by a fairy and discovered by the prince, thanks to a slipper. But, unlike Cinderella, there were many more trials ahead for Tam before she and her prince could live happily ever after.

I met Thumbelina, too, in the person of Little Finger. Her adventures were very different from Hans Christian Andersen's tiny heroine, yet she too was lost in a forest and at last became a queen.

I knew Tu Thuc for some time before I recognized him as Rip Van Winkle. The fairies he met were of a gentler sort than the dwarfs of the Catskills, yet the world he returned to was even more altered than was Rip Van Winkle's.

The Frog Prince's adventures seem somewhat pale beside Master Frog's: winning the princess did not automatically rid him of his ugly skin. In Vietnamese fairy tales one usually must work hard to deserve to "live happily ever after."

Fairy tale princesses, whether of the West or East, are not often found in servant's garb surrounded by geese. Yet it happened to the Grimms brothers' Goose Girl, and it happened to Quynh Dao. Each lost her royal identity on the way to marry her prince, and each in the end triumphed over her oppressor.

Five familiar faces in an unfamiliar land; it is fascinating that similar ideas have arisen and then developed into different stories under the influence of two such diverse cultures as East and West. Perhaps it is a testimony to the fact that we are each uniquely individual, with rich ethnic identities, yet bound together by a common humanity.

In preparing these stories I have made use of a number of sources. The series *Chuyện Nhi Đồng Việt-Nam* (Vietnamese Children's Stories) by Tô Lan Chi (Saigon, 1964), the series of children's picture books written by Phi Sơn and illustrated by Hoàng Lương (Hồng Dân Book Company, Saigon, 1964), and *Việt-Nam Văn-Học Toàn Thư* (The Complete Literature of Viet-Nam) by Hoàng Trộng Miên, Volume II (Legends), (Văn Hữu Á Châu Publishing Company, Saigon, 1959) were particularly helpful. I have also referred to Nguyễn Duy's *Truyện Cổ Việt-Nam* (Old Stories of Viet-Nam: Bốn Phương Publishers, Saigon, 1940), Vũ Bằng's *Cổ-Tích Việt-Nam* (Vietnamese Legends), Book I (P. Văn Tươi Publishing Company, Saigon, 1956), *Chuyện Đời Xưa* (Stories of Long Ago) by Trương Vĩnh Ký (Khai Trí Book Company, Saigon), and *Chuyện Xưa Tích Cũ* (Ancient Tales, Old Legends), Volume IV, by Tô Nguyệt Đình (Rạng Đông Publishing Company, Saigon). This list of acknowledgments would not be complete if I did not include my husband. My first Vietnamese teacher and "unabridged dictionary," his suggestions and criticisms have proved invaluable throughout this project.

The Brocaded Slipper

<small>◆⇒◎⇐◆</small>

I<small>N OLDEN TIMES THERE</small>
lived a man whose wife had died leaving him with
their only child, a beautiful daughter named Tam.
Some time afterwards, the man married again. His
second wife was a widow who also had a daughter
of her own, an ugly ungainly girl named Cam.
The stepmother was a cruel woman and hated Tam
for her beauty and sweet disposition. Not many
years later, Tam's father also died. From that time
on, she was treated little better than a servant,
working long hours both in the kitchen and in the
fields, as well as tending the water buffaloes and

other animals, while Cam spent the day lazily at home with her mother. Tam did not dare to complain at this unjust treatment, so greatly did she fear her stepmother's beatings.

One morning after breakfast the stepmother called the two girls and handed each of them a basket and a pail.

"Go down to the pond and get these baskets filled by noon," she said. "The one who brings home the most fish will have a new red blouse."

Tam could hardly believe her ears. As the two girls turned to leave, she looked down at her worn pants and patched top. A new red blouse! She could scarcely remember when she had last had something new. She ran down the path, Cam ambling along behind.

As soon as they reached the water's edge, Tam set to work, damming up the channel that led from the pond to the river. Cam glanced after her with a yawn, then tossed her basket under a tree and lay down in the shade.

Tam lowered her pail into the water and began to drain the pond, dipping out bucketful after bucketful until nothing but mud oozed beneath her feet. Now she could see the fish, their bodies flapping frantically as they burrowed into the slime.

Tam dived after them, digging for them in the soft, wet mud, tossing them one by one into her basket.

The sun was high overhead when Tam set down her basket, filled to the brim, at the side of the pond and reopened the channel. Cam stretched lazily and rose to her feet, walking down to the water's edge.

"What a mess you are!" she called as Tam glanced up at her. "You'd better wash up before we go home."

But as soon as Tam stepped down into the river, Cam hurriedly poured all her sister's fish into her own empty basket and ran off with it.

Tam raised her head and looked around for Cam, but she was already out of sight. Then her eyes lighted on her basket, lying empty on the ground. What would her stepmother say? She winced, remembering the sting of the bamboo stick on her back. She covered her face with her hands, and tears of fear and frustration slipped through her fingers.

Suddenly she felt someone touch her shoulder. Looking up, she saw a fairy standing beside her.

"Why are you crying, my child?" the fairy asked her.

Tam pointed to the basket. "My sister's stolen

all my fish, and I don't dare go home empty-handed."

The fairy picked up the basket and handed it to her.

"Look again. Are you sure it's empty?"

To her amazement, Tam saw a fat little fish lying at the bottom.

"This fish is worth more than all the ones you've lost," the fairy consoled her. "Take him home at once and put him in the well. He'll bring you good luck."

Before Tam could thank her, the fairy had vanished, and Tam ran home to do as she had been instructed. After every meal Tam set aside a few grains of rice and slipped out to the well with them. Then, making certain that no one was watching, she knelt by the side of the well and called the fish. As soon as he heard her voice, he would come to the surface and gobble up the rice that she threw to him.

As time went by, the fish grew bigger and bigger, and Tam came to love him more and more. But one day Cam noticed that Tam left a few grains of rice in her bowl. When she saw her scoop them up in her hand and slip out the door with them, Cam's curiosity was aroused. Stealthily she followed her out of the house and hid behind a tree to see what would happen.

She heard her call the fish:

> *Come and eat, come and eat*
> *Little fish, pretty fish.*
> *Good rice, fine rice,*
> *From my gold and silver dish.*

Repeating the little verse to herself, Cam hurried back to the house to tell her mother.

"Wasting good rice on a fish?" the woman grunted when she heard the story. "Well, let's hope it's big enough to make a meal for the two of us."

The next morning as Tam was leaving the house to tend the buffaloes, her stepmother stopped her.

"The grass near here is getting rather sparse," she said. "Take the buffaloes down to the bend in the river today." She handed her a square of pressed rice wrapped in banana leaves. "Here's your lunch. Be sure you get the herd back by sundown."

Shortly before noon Cam took some rice out to the well and, imitating her sister, called the fish. When it came to the surface, she speared it with a pointed stick and took it into the house for her mother to cook.

That evening, right after supper, Tam hurried out to the well. She had saved more rice than usual to make up for the noon meal, which her pet had missed. Though she called the fish again and again, there was no sign of him.

Someone was standing beside her. Looking up, she saw the fairy.

"Oh, dear fairy," she cried, tears springing to her eyes, "my fish is gone. Do you know where he is?"

"Your stepsister killed and ate him," she told her gently. "But don't be sad. He will still bring you good luck. Now you must go and find his bones at once. When you've found them, divide them into four parts and place them in four jars, which you must bury — one under each of the corners of your bed. After one hundred days, dig them up again."

Before she could question her further, the fairy had vanished. Tam felt perplexed, wondering where to look for the bones and not daring to ask her stepmother or sister.

A rooster pecking away at the ground nearby suddenly started to crow.

Cock-a-doodle-doo. Cock-a-doodle-doo.
Give me the rice, and I'll find the bones for you.

Tam quickly threw the rice to him and waited impatiently while he snapped it up grain by grain. Then he led her over to a pile of garbage and, scratching away, soon uncovered the missing bones.

Tam gathered them up and ran off to find the jars. That night, after her stepmother and sister were sleeping, she dug four holes in the dirt floor — one under each corner of her bed — and buried them.

Oh how the next three months dragged by as Tam counted off the days the fairy had prescribed! At last the hundredth day arrived. That night Tam went to bed early, lying awake in the darkness until her stepmother and sister had retired. As soon as she was sure they were asleep, she slipped out of bed and crept out of the house to get the shovel.

Scarcely able to contain her excitement, she dug away the earth, uncovering first one jar and then another, filling in each hole again carefully. Then she squatted down to open the jars. As she lifted the cover of the first one, she gasped. She could see something sparkling at the bottom of it.

She . . . pulled them out again for one last look . . .

Nàng . . . đem đôi hài ra để nhìn thêm một lần cuối . . .

Reaching in, she pulled out a pair of red brocaded slippers. She ran to the window and examined them in the moonlight, stroking the rich silk material and gently running her fingers over the golden phoenixes that decorated them. She slipped them on her feet. How comfortable they were! A perfect fit!

Hurrying back to the other jars, she opened them. From one she pulled out a beautiful dress and from the others gold and silver and jewels of every description. She scooped them up in her hands, marveling that the world could contain such lovely objects. The profusion of stones sparkled in the moonlight and dazzled her. Reluctantly she put the covers back on the jars and shoved them under the bed. She had no place to wear such finery. She took off the slippers and started to put them away as well, then pulled them out again for one last look at the golden phoenixes. No, she couldn't bear to let them out of her sight. Finally she slipped them under her pillow and lay down to sleep.

The next morning Tam put them on. She gazed down at her feet, admiring their beauty in the early morning sunlight. True, they looked rather out of place with her simple black country garb, but she didn't care. She would wear them now wherever she went.

Tam breathed deeply, inhaling the fresh morning air as she walked along, driving the buffaloes to pasture. The rocky path beneath her feet might have been clouds, so light were her spirits that morning.

Suddenly she stumbled. Her foot had slipped into a puddle. Oh, her beautiful slippers! The golden phoenixes were black with mud. She pulled them off and hurried to a little stream nearby. Kneeling down, she dipped them in the water, carefully washing away the dirt. Then she hung them to dry on the horns of one of her buffaloes and sat down on a rock to rest.

All at once the air was filled with a cawing sound. Crows were flying overhead. One of them dipped suddenly, snatched up a slipper in his beak, and flew off with it. Tam screamed, chasing after him till he was out of sight, but to no avail. There was no way she could get her slipper back.

The crow flew on and on until it came to the capital, where the king lived. The crown prince was strolling through his garden that morning when suddenly a bird flew overhead, dropping a bright red object at his feet. Startled, the prince bent over and picked it up. It was a brocaded slipper, the finest and most delicately made he had ever seen. He turned it over and over in his hands, marveling at its small size and skilled workmanship.

"This must belong to some beautiful princess," he mused. "How I would like to meet her!"

The more he looked at the slipper, the more fascinated he became with it. He could not get it out of his mind, nor could he concentrate on anything else. All he could think of was how he could find the girl who had worn that enchanting slipper.

Meanwhile the king had decided it was time for his son to have a wife. But when he suggested different princesses to him, the prince only shook his head sadly.

"I know who I want to marry," he told his father, "but I don't know where to find her." He drew out the brocaded slipper, which he had hidden in his robe. "I've made up my mind to marry no one but the owner of this slipper."

A few days later a huge celebration was proclaimed throughout the kingdom, inviting all the young women to come and try on the brocaded slipper. The girl whose foot fit the slipper perfectly would become the prince's bride.

"Cam and I will go first," the stepmother told Tam when they heard the news. "You can come after us as soon as you finish a little job I have for you. I've set two bushels of sesame seeds outside, and I want you to sort them. Put the black seeds in one basket and the white ones in another."

In despair, Tam walked out of the house and sat down in front of the baskets. What was the use of even trying such an impossible task? By the time she finished, the celebration would be over. She buried her face in her hands, and the tears flowed through her fingers. Suddenly she felt something brush against her shoulder. A flock of pigeons had lighted on the rims of the baskets and were sorting the seeds. Tam watched in amazement at the speed with which they worked. In no time at all, the white seeds were in one basket and the black ones in another.

As soon as the birds had flown away, Tam hurried into the house to get dressed. Now at last she could wear all the beautiful things that were hidden under her bed. She wrapped up the slipper that was left and, putting it in the front of her dress, set off for the celebration.

The hall was filled with people when she arrived, and guards stood at the door to direct the young women who had come. One of them led her over to where a large crowd had gathered. As she approached, she heard her stepmother's voice.

"Pull it a little more, Cam," she was saying. "Maybe you can get it on."

"It's plain it's not her shoe," the prince objected. "Take it off before you rip the seams."

The guard led Tam forward. The prince looked at her, his eyes lighting up.

"Let her try the slipper next," he ordered.

The stepmother sneered at Tam. "What are you doing here? How could a worthless girl like you get it on if Cam couldn't?"

Tam took the slipper in her hand and put it on her foot. Then she pulled a small parcel out of her dress and unwrapped it.

The prince sprang from his seat as she slid her foot into the other slipper.

"The search is over," he exclaimed, gently raising her to her feet. "I've found my bride."

Not long after, their wedding was celebrated amid the rejoicing of all the people of the kingdom — except Cam and her mother. In their jealousy and anger, they began to plot how they could get rid of Tam.

"If only she were out of the way," the stepmother muttered, "my Cam might be able to take her place."

Weeks and months passed. On the anniversary of her father's death, Tam went home for the ceremony in his memory. As soon as she arrived, she went out to the kitchen to help with the dinner.

But her stepmother stopped her. "After all, you're a princess now," she said. "But there is one thing you can do for us. Would you get us some areca nuts? You're so much more agile than we are."

Tam went out to the garden at once. Grasping the trunk of the areca palm, she pulled herself up as Cam and her mother, an ax behind her back, watched from the ground.

Higher and higher Tam climbed, until the nuts were within reach. Suddenly the tree was shaking violently. Letting go of the nuts, Tam wrapped her arms around the trunk in alarm.

"What's happening?" she cried.

"Don't worry, daughter," her stepmother replied, as she swung the ax at the tree again, "it's only me, chasing away the ants."

The tree trembled under the repeated blows. Terrified, Tam clung to the slender trunk as she felt it give way. Then suddenly the tree fell to the ground, carrying Tam with it. She was killed instantly, but her soul flew off in the form of an oriole.

Cam's mother looked at her daughter in satisfaction. "Put on your best clothes," she ordered. "We're going to the palace."

With tears in their eyes, Cam and her mother asked to see the prince and, between sobs, told him that Tam's death had been an accident.

"What a thing to have happen on the anniversary of my husband's passing!" the woman wailed. "And such a dutiful daughter. She remembered how much her father had liked areca nuts." She wiped a tear from her eye. "I didn't want her to climb that tree, but she insisted. If only she'd been more careful!"

The prince was so overcome with shock that he could scarcely answer. Tears of sorrow ran down his cheeks as the stepmother continued:

"And so, Your Highness, I've come to ask you to please accept Tam's younger sister in her place. I know she will be but poor consolation for you, but I'm sure Tam would want it that way."

The prince shuddered at the ugliness of the girl,

but for Tam's sake he agreed to let her stay. In his heart, however, he still pined for Tam and paid little attention to Cam.

One day Cam was sitting in the window overlooking the garden, where a servant was washing the prince's clothes. Suddenly an oriole flew into the garden, perched on the hedge, and began to sing:

> *Chirp, chirp!*
> *Who's washing my husband's shirt?*
> *Wash it white, hang it right.*
> *If you tear it, how can he wear it?*

Inside the palace the prince heard her song and stepped outside to see the bird. His heart beat fast as he called to her:

> *Oriole, O golden bird,*
> *Give a sign to prove your word.*
> *Fly into my open sleeve;*
> *Come, my sorrowing heart relieve.*

As he raised his arm, the bird left the hedge and flew straight to him, lighting inside his long flowing sleeve. Overjoyed, the prince took her in

As he raised his arm, the bird left the hedge and flew straight to him . . .

Thái-tử vừa đưa tay lên, chim vội bỏ hàng rào bay đến chàng . . .

his hands, gently stroking her smooth golden feathers.

"Beautiful little bird," he crooned. "Now I know you're my lost Tam. I'll build a golden cage for you and keep you near me always."

Cam watched jealously from the window.

"Will I never be rid of that girl?" she muttered.

A few days later when the prince was gone, Cam killed the bird and cooked it. Not wishing any of the servants to see her, she went out to the garden to eat it, tossing away the bones as she finished. That evening when the prince returned home, he found Cam weeping beside the empty cage.

"I opened the door only for a moment to put in fresh water," she sobbed. "But the bird flew out, and the cat got her before I could stop him." She buried her face in her handkerchief. "If only I'd been more careful! I'll never forgive myself."

Seeing her sorrow, the prince did not have the heart to scold her, grief-stricken though he was. With head bowed sadly, he walked out to the garden. Up and down among the rows of flowers he drifted, pausing now and then before one that Tam had loved. Suddenly his eyes caught sight of two peach trees which had not been there before. How could two such lovely trees have sprung up without his knowledge?

He walked closer, turning first to one tree and then to the other, wondering. The leaves were murmuring in the breeze. He stopped short. Had he heard Tam's voice, or was it only his imagination? Overcome with emotion, he threw his arms around the trunk. The leaves bent down and brushed against his neck and cheeks.

"My dear lost Tam," the prince cried, gently

stroking the smooth bark. "I've found you again."

That evening he hung his hammock between the two peach trees, and from then on he spent all of his spare time there.

Day after day Cam sat in the palace, watching him from her window. Anger filled her heart that he should prefer a tree to her. Why had she been so careless with those bones? If only she were rid of Tam completely, perhaps she would have a chance of winning the prince's love.

At last the day that Cam was waiting for arrived. The prince set off on a mission for his father, not to return for several days. As soon as he was gone, Cam called the servants and ordered them to chop down the two peach trees.

"Dig out the stumps and burn them," she said. "Then take the wood and have it made into a loom for me."

"Now you shall serve me," Cam gloated when the loom was brought to her. "I have you in my power at last. The prince could pet a bird, and he could enjoy the shade of a tree." She put her head back, laughing evilly. "But what use would he have for a loom?"

Taking a skein of silk she unwound it onto the loom to form the warp. Then she sat down and began to pass the shuttle back and forth between the threads.

"Hah!" she thought. "Soon I'll have a beautiful new dress — so beautiful that the prince will have to notice me." She gave the loom frame a slap. "Dear, sweet sister Tam! How kind of you to do this for me."

"Clackety–clack–clack," answered the loom.

A chill passed over Cam. The creaking of the loom had sounded strangely like Tam's voice. She passed the shuttle through again, pushing down the woof threads.

> *Clackety-clack-clack-clack!*
> *Give my husband back.*
> *Or your head I'll crack.*

Cam ran to the window for a breath of fresh air. She couldn't have heard it. Of course she was only imagining things. She gulped down a cup of hot tea and went back to the loom.

> *Clackety-clack-clack-clack!*
> *Give my husband back. . . .*

In a frenzy she threw the shuttle out the window. Her eyes lighted on one of the prince's swords hanging on the wall. She grabbed it wildly, hacking away at the loom. One of the servants found her later, lying beside a heap of useless wood.

"Take it away," she shrieked. "Burn it and throw the ashes outside the city walls. Don't throw them in the garden if you value your life!"

Frightened, the servant did as she said. That very day the ashes were taken and thrown along a country road far from the city.

The next morning an old woman walking that way stopped in surprise when she saw a beautiful persimmon tree growing by the side of the road.

"Strange," she muttered to herself. "I've never noticed that tree before. And what a luscious-looking fruit!" There was only one, its green coat just beginning to change to golden yellow. "If only I could reach it." No sooner were the words spoken than the persimmon fell from the branch, landing in her basket.

How happy the old woman was! She rushed home and put it in her rice jar to ripen.

The next day when she returned home from market, she could hardly believe her eyes. During her absence, someone had come into the house and swept it clean. The clothes had been washed and were drying outside. A rice bowl and a pair of chopsticks had been set out for her, and a delicious meal was prepared and ready to be eaten. There was even a fresh pot of tea, and several chews of betel had been rolled. She ran from one corner to another of the cottage, exclaiming at each new discovery.

"Someone must have come in while I was gone," she mused. "But who — in this deserted place?"

The next morning when she went out, she closed all the shutters carefully and locked the door behind her. But later when she returned, all the housework had been done as before.

"Could there be a fairy in my house?" the old woman wondered. "I must get to the bottom of this mystery."

The next day she set off for market as usual, her basket over her arm. But after she had gone down the road a way, she turned around and walked back to the house. Hiding behind the door, she peeked in through a crack. Suddenly she saw the rice jar open and a beautiful girl step out. As the old woman tiptoed back into the house, the girl turned her head and saw her. She ran toward the rice jar, but the old woman grabbed her arm before she could escape.

"Who are you?" the woman cried. "Where did you come from?"

"I have been many things," Tam replied. "First I was a poor country girl, an orphan; but later I became a princess, thanks to a fairy's kindness. But my stepmother and sister killed me out of jealousy. Then my spirit entered the body of a bird, but again my stepsister killed me. The bones grew into two peach trees, but once more she destroyed me. Finally I became the persimmon which fell into your basket a few days ago. Now thanks to your catching me today, I'm free at last and can resume human form." Tam fell on her knees. "I will always honor you as my mother."

The old woman raised her gently to her feet. "I'm happy to have you as my daughter!" she said.

That evening when the woman opened the rice jar there was nothing left of the persimmon but its skin. As she broke it, it disappeared in her hands.

From that day on, Tam and the old woman lived together in the little house. Tam loved the rustic serenity of their country life, yet her heart longed for the prince.

Back at the palace, the prince returned home

to find that his peach trees had vanished. Nowhere could he find their wood; and though he searched the garden from one end to the other, there was no trace of his lost wife. Heartbroken, he decided to go on a hunting trip to forget his sorrow. Early the next morning he set off with his companions, traveling the road that led from the city to a distant forest. There were few houses along the way; so about noon, when they saw a cottage across the field, they decided to stop for a rest.

The old woman greeted the prince and his company and led them inside.

"Gentlemen, please come in and have some tea," she invited them. "My house is poor, but strangers are always welcome."

"Your kindness will be amply rewarded," the prince replied, as she set bowls of rice and fish in front of them.

After they had finished eating, she brought betel for them to chew. The prince picked up the green leaf skillfully rolled around the piece of areca nut and stared at it in amazement. He had never seen anyone prepare betel so well except his lost Tam. Even the lime was applied exactly as she used to do it.

"Grandmother," the prince addressed the old woman, "please tell me who prepared this betel."

Just then Tam stepped into the room. The prince rushed to her side and took her in his arms, oblivious of the stares of his companions.

"My Tam!" he cried. "I've found you at last."

How happy the old woman was at the unexpected reunion.

"Please stay tonight," she begged. "Let me prepare a dinner to celebrate this joyous occasion."

The next morning the prince sent for a sedan chair to bring Tam back to the palace. When Cam looked out of her window and saw Tam approaching, she was filled with fear. Three times she had killed her stepsister; now that she was returning, she would surely have her revenge. Terror-stricken, her exit from the door blocked off, she crawled out of a window and ran toward the garden wall. Slowly, painfully, she pulled herself up the stone surface. Then, as she reached the top, her foot caught in a crevice, and she lost her balance. Falling to the ground below, she was killed as her head hit a rock.

But Tam, whose many trials had only made her more beautiful, lived happily with the prince for many years, loved by all the people of the kingdom, first as their princess and later as their queen.

Little Finger
of the
Watermelon Patch

⟡━━◦◦━━⟡

There was once a poor woodcutter and his wife who had longed for many years for a child. Finally a tiny little girl was born to them.

"She's no ordinary child," her father declared when he saw how small she was. "She must have come from the fairy world."

His wife nodded as she stroked the tiny form beside her on the pillow. "Why, she's no bigger than your little finger," she said.

And from that day the child was known as Little Finger.

As soon as she was old enough, they began to

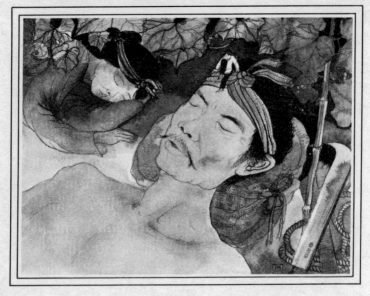

. . . the three of them ate their fill of the ripe fruit and then
lay down for a nap.

. . . cả ba ăn dưa no rồi tìm chỗ ngủ trưa.

take her along with them when they went to the
forest to cut wood. Each morning they set out,
with ax in hand and Little Finger secured in the
folds of the cloth that her father tied around
his head.

One day while they were looking for a place
to eat their lunch, they came upon a watermelon
patch. Overjoyed at their find, the three of them

ate their fill of the ripe fruit and then lay down for a nap.

As soon as her parents were asleep, Little Finger crawled out of her father's turban and stood up on his forehead to look around. How smooth those big green watermelons looked! What fun it would be to climb to the top of one and slide down. And those lovely vines! Just right for swinging, and some of them were low enough for her to reach.

Little Finger slid down the side of her father's head and started off. The tall grass tickled her nose, but she brushed it aside and hurried on, not noticing the bamboo poles that lay about on the ground. She tripped over one and fell flat on her face, ripping her pants and skinning her knee on a rough joint.

Suddenly she heard a low growl. A big black bear with her two cubs was coming toward the watermelon patch. Her heart beating wildly, Little Finger crawled into the bamboo pole. She lay in the darkness, listening for the sound of the bears passing by. How tired she felt. She yawned once and then again; her eyelids closed drowsily.

The bears feasted on the ripe watermelon and

then, their stomachs full, lumbered off into the forest just as Little Finger's parents awoke.

"Little Finger!" the wife cried suddenly, pointing to her husband's head. "She's gone!"

They sprang to their feet, running to and fro among the watermelons searching for her, calling her name.

Finally their eyes lighted on the bamboo pole. Something black was stuck in one of the cracks, and the breeze caught it and blew it about. The woodcutter and his wife knelt down to examine it. It was a piece of Little Finger's pants. And bear tracks were on both sides of the pole. They rose to their feet slowly, tears in their eyes. The bears had gotten Little Finger. Their hearts heavy with sorrow, they walked back for their ax and the bundle of wood, and then trudged off through the woods for home.

Little Finger stretched and then opened her eyes, slowly remembering where she was. She wriggled her way to the end of the bamboo pole and peered out. Where were her parents? She crawled out and stood up on her tiptoes, calling them.

Shivering with the cold of the night breeze,

shuddering at the strange shapes and sounds in the darkness, she called again and again. But the only answer was the sound of the wind rustling through the trees and the hooting of the owls as they flew by overhead. Finally she crawled back into the bamboo pole and lay down again. It was too dark for Father and Mother to find her now, but they would be back for her tomorrow.

Bright and early the next morning, Little Finger was up and out of the bamboo pole. All morning long she waited, calling for her parents again and again, until the hot sun drove her under the shade of the watermelon vines. But when evening came, no one had come to fetch her. That night Little Finger cried herself to sleep, curled up inside the bamboo pole.

The days stretched into weeks and weeks into months, and still she waited. The watermelons and other plants that grew nearby kept her well supplied with food, and at night she slept inside the bamboo pole to protect herself from the wild animals. The years went by, and Little Finger grew until she was as big as a small corncob.

Meanwhile, far away in the big city, the old king had decided it was time to choose one of his three sons to take his place.

"But first I must know which of you is worthy to succeed me," he told them. "So I am sending each of you out to find a wife for yourself. When I see how well you have chosen, I will know who is the wisest and which one should be king after me."

The three princes bade their father farewell, mounted their horses, and set out as he had commanded.

"Why don't you take the left fork, Hau," the oldest prince suggested to the youngest when they reached a place where the main highway branched into two smaller roads.

"We might as well separate right here," agreed the second. "You know you can never keep up with us. Remember the time you stopped to pick up that bird with the broken wing?"

"And on the way back from our last hunting trip," the oldest broke in, "you stopped to feed that mangy old dog with your share of the meat! You will be much better off by yourself, and we won't have to be hurrying you all the time."

The two brothers exchanged a knowing grin. Of course, the winner would be one of them. That younger brother of theirs was too stupid to win anything. Some people said he was just soft-

32

hearted. Soft–headed would be a better word, they thought. And the left fork led to the forest. What kind of wife would he find in there? A mangy one with broken wings, most likely!

Hau steered his horse down the road that led to the forest. Those brothers of his always made him feel like he was such a bother. So it was probably just as well they had wanted to go alone. It was better to be by himself than to have them making fun of him all the time.

The sun was high in the sky and getting hot, and he was thirsty. He hurried his horse toward the shade up ahead, winding his way along the path through the trees. It must be nearly noon. He smiled as he thought of the good lunch in his pouch—the thick slabs of roast meat and the rice pressed into cakes.

Say, were those watermelons over there? He drew his horse to a stop and dismounted, then took his knife from his side and severed the fruit from the vine. He sliced off a piece and began to eat. It was delicious. He flung away the rind and started to cut another slice.

Suddenly he heard a cry. He stopped, the knife clutched in his hand, and looked about him in

A tiny girl, no bigger than an ear of corn, lay huddled on the ground . . .

Một cô bé tí-hon không lớn hơn một trái bắp nằm co dưới đất . . .

alarm. It had sounded almost human! And it had come from the direction in which he had tossed the watermelon rind.

He stood up and walked toward the patch of vines. A soft moaning seemed to be coming from under the leaves. He brushed them aside and stared in amazement. A tiny girl, no bigger than an ear of corn, lay huddled on the ground, holding her shoulder and groaning. His watermelon rind lay next to her.

"I'm sorry I hit you," he said gently. He picked her up and set her on his palm. "Does it still hurt very badly?"

"N...no," she stammered. Then she drew herself up to her full height and faced him, her hands on her hips. "But who are you? And what are you doing in my watermelon patch?"

"My name is Hau, and I am the king's youngest son." He reached into his pouch and drew out a coin. "I didn't know the watermelons were yours. Will this be enough for the one I took?"

She laughed and sat down again on his hand. "Oh, you needn't pay me for the watermelon. What could I do with the money anyway?"

"Have you always lived here?" he asked her.

"You are awfully small to be all by yourself. Where is your home?"

The tears came to her eyes. "I don't know," she told him. And she sobbed out the whole story for Hau to hear.

"You poor little thing," he sympathized as she finished. "I'll help you find your father and mother. But first, let's have something to eat." He set her down on his knee and opened his pouch. They finished their lunch, then wiped their hands clean on watermelon leaves.

"Now tell me which way to go," Hau said, setting Little Finger on his shoulder and mounting his horse, "and we will have you home with your parents in no time."

"B...but, sir," she stammered, "I don't know the way out of the forest."

"But where did you live?"

"In a great big hut with a thatched roof and coconut palms around it, in the middle of a big rice field."

Hau sighed. How many thatched-roofed huts must there be in the country? And how many coconut palms and rice fields and woodcutters? He would have to take her back to the palace and have heralds sent up and down throughout the countryside to search for her parents. He could set out again tomorrow to look for a wife.

It was evening by the time they reached the palace. Hau gasped in astonishment as they rode into the courtyard. Everywhere brightly colored lanterns, strung from one end to the other, lighted up the night like an army of fireflies. Gaily festooned banners and streamers crisscrossed the garden.

Then a cheer went up from the crowd at the other end of the courtyard. "Prince Hau is home!"

He saw his brothers, each with a beautiful girl by his side. They stared at Hau as he approached. Then suddenly the oldest burst out laughing.

"Look at him! Look at the wife he's brought home!"

"Where did you find her?" sneered the second. "Did you find her in a cornfield?"

"Aren't you afraid you will step on her?"

"Hold on there, midget. I feel a sneeze coming on."

"Now that will be enough," the king interrupted them. "If this is the girl your brother has chosen, there must be more to her than meets the eye."

"I should hope so!" the oldest prince snickered

in an undertone to the second. But the king's stern look stopped them.

"Father, please, I . . ." Hau began.

The king smiled at him and at Little Finger perched on Hau's shoulder. "It's all right, son," he said kindly. "If this is the girl you have chosen, I feel certain she will prove her worth. Your brothers got home just before you did, and we were only waiting for you to begin the wedding celebration. So tonight we'll be merry, and tomorrow each of my new daughters will present me with a meal so that I may see which is the most talented."

The king gave the signal to strike up the band, and the fun began. For all except poor Hau. There wouldn't be any chance to talk to his father tonight. He would go and see him the first thing tomorrow morning and tell him what had happened.

The next morning Hau awoke with a start to find the sun already streaming through the window. He turned toward the chest and saw Little Finger sitting on top of it, next to the pincushion that he had found for her pillow the night before. She smiled as she caught his eye.

"Your tray is over there on the table," she told him. "I would have taken it myself, but it's really quite heavy, and I don't believe I could manage it."

With a gasp of astonishment he sprang from the bed, ran to the table, and lifted the cover. Under it lay a delicious-looking meal of roast duck, fried rice, and asparagus soup. He turned to Little Finger in amazement, a thousand questions rushing to his lips.

She was still smiling. "Please don't ask me anything now. Just hurry and take the tray to the king. You don't want to miss your chance to win."

Everyone had gathered in the dining hall by the time Hau and Little Finger arrived. The meals prepared by the other two girls were on the table, and the king was sampling them. Silently Hau laid his own tray down beside theirs.

As the king removed the cover, everyone gasped in astonishment. The king picked up a piece of meat with his chopsticks and put it in his mouth.

"Take the other meals to the kitchen," he commanded, slurping a mouthful of soup from the china spoon. "This is the one I want to eat." At last he leaned back in his chair, patting his stomach contentedly. "There is no doubt about it," he said, turning to Hau. "You will be the next king."

"But, Father," the eldest son broke in. "Cooking is not the only accomplishment a girl should have."

The second son agreed. "A girl should be able to sew, too."

"All right," nodded the king. "Then let's see which of you can bring me the best robe tomorrow morning. And in the meantime, I do not want to be bothered by any of you."

He rose and left the room, followed by his attendants. Well, that was that, Hau thought, discouraged. For a minute, it had looked as if he would win after all. But his brothers had fixed that, like they always did. Even if Little Finger did know how to make a robe, she would never be able to finish it by tomorrow morning — as little as she was!

But the next morning Little Finger was sitting on the chest next to a neatly folded garment of blue and gold brocade almost as high as she was.

Awestruck, Hau picked it up, letting the rich material fall into shimmering folds. Where had she found such material? He had never seen such beautiful golden dragons.

"It's lovely! It's wonderful," he murmured, at a loss for words. "I don't know how you managed it, and I don't know how to thank you." Perhaps his father had been right. Perhaps there was more to Little Finger than met the eye.

The brothers were just ahead of him. Hau took a quick glance at the robes they were carrying and couldn't help feeling a surge of pride in the loveliness of his own offering.

The eldest son walked forward and presented his robe to his father. The king unfolded it and drew it on, tying it at the waist.

"A little long in the sleeves," he commented, holding his arms out, "but otherwise not bad."

He took it off and reached for the second son's robe.

"Fairly good workmanship," he conceded as he handed it back to him, "but rather tight under the arms."

His eyes lighted up as he saw the robe that Hau was holding out to him.

"Beautiful!" he murmured, smoothing his hands over the brocade. "Here's one that's fit for an emperor." He slipped it on eagerly. "I've never worn anything so comfortable." He sat down on his throne, adjusting the robe around him. "That settles it. The throne belongs to my third son."

"But, Father," the first son objected. "It's only fair that we should be judged in three categories."

"Yes, Father," the second chimed in. "Shouldn't the girl herself count for something?"

"All right then," their father agreed. "We'll have one more contest, and that'll be the end of it. Tomorrow morning the prize will go to whichever of my daughters can prove herself the most beautiful and charming. And now out of my sight, all of you, and leave me in peace for the rest of the day."

Hau turned to leave with a heavy heart. Well, that was the end of it. Of course it wasn't fair. But his brothers always managed to get what they wanted, no matter what happened.

Hau slept fitfully that night; dawn was just breaking when he opened his eyes and saw a beautiful girl standing by his bedside. She looked like Little Finger! He glanced over at the chest. There was nothing there but the vase of flowers and the little pincushion pillow.

She smiled at him as he sat up.

"Yes, I'm Little Finger," she told him. "I'm a fairy, and I was banished to earth for breaking a precious vase. Only the day before yesterday my sentence was finished, and I began to regain my power. And now I'm allowed to return to my true form." She took his hand and drew him to his feet. "Come, let's be the first ones today. The new king shouldn't arrive late."

Everyone was filled with astonishment when they saw Hau and Little Finger. And for once the two older princes were shocked into speechlessness. The old king rose from his throne and called Hau to him.

"Here is my successor," he announced, drawing his signet ring from his hand and placing it on Hau's finger.

The whole court cheered for Hau and his queen. That day marked the beginning of a long reign of peace and prosperity, filled with joy for Hau and Little Finger and happiness for their people. And not long afterward Little Finger sent for her parents and had them brought to the palace, where they spent many happy years with their daughter and son-in-law.

The Fairy Grotto

◆═◎═◆

TU THUC GLANCED UP from the pile of papers at the anxious face of the woman before him. He waited patiently as she shifted her baby to her other hip and fumbled in the sash tied around her plain brown tunic. Finally she drew out a small, cloth money bag, shook out the two copper coins, and laid them in his hand.

"Please, sir, now that my husband is dead, it's all I have." The eyes in the gaunt face pleaded with him. "Please give me a few more months — till the next harvest. Don't let them take my field and sell it."

"Hmm. How much do you owe?" Tu Thuc reached for the tax register.

The lines in her forehead deepened. "Ten coppers, sir."

Yes, here it was: Lam Tai's widow. His fingers pinpointed the entry. Life was not easy for a woman alone. But what did the courts care? The law was the law. But somehow he couldn't brush people aside without caring.

Keeping a finger at the corner of the page, he closed the register, then pressed the two coins back into the woman's hand. "According to the record your account was settled last month."

The tears sprang to her eyes. "Sir, you must be mistaken!" She dabbed at her cheeks with the towel that hung from under her conical straw hat. "Oh, sir. Thank you. Thank you," she said, as she realized Tu Thuc's generous gesture. She drew the tail of her tunic around her baby and ran from the room.

Tu Thuc opened the register again, dipped his brush in the ink, and marked "paid in full" after the entry. Then he reached for his money pouch, counted out ten coppers, and unlocking the money chest, placed them inside.

He sighed as he sat down again at the table

and drew the pile of papers toward him. If only all his problems as district chief were so easy to solve! Too often there was little he could do about the injustice and human suffering he saw day by day. But when it was within his power, he would do what he could.

He turned one sheet after another, making a notation here, adding his signature there, scarcely noticing the passing time till the light from the window had dimmed to near darkness.

With a start he realized how late it had grown. Today was the day of the Flower Festival — the day when people came from all over the countryside to visit the temple gardens and to celebrate the beauty of springtime. Of course, the main attraction would be, as it always was, the giant peonies that bloomed like flowers from fairyland on the bush that had suddenly sprung up some years before beside the entrance to the temple. Tu Thuc drew his brocade coat over his mandarin robes and hurried outside.

Crowds still thronged the garden when he reached it. The sweet scent of the flowers drew him onward from one lovely blossom to another as he stopped to admire each one in turn.

Suddenly angry voices filled the air — rough

At her feet lay a branch broken from the peony . . .

Một cành hoa mẫu-đơn . . . nằm ngay cạnh chân nàng.

shouts and, nearly drowned out by them, a girl's cries. Bewildered he rushed toward the uproar, straight to the steps of the temple. A young girl, breathtakingly beautiful in spite of her tear-stained face and disheveled hair, was struggling in the grasp of two temple guards who had pinned her arms to her sides and were tying her wrists behind her. At her feet lay a branch broken from the peony, its magnificent rainbow-colored blossoms covered with dust.

"Sir, we saw her do it," one of the guards answered Tu Thuc's question. "She purposely broke off the branch and would have made off with it if we hadn't stopped her."

"It's not true. It's not true!" the girl cried. "Even if I had wanted to, how could I have dared to do such a thing with so many people watching me?" She broke into fresh sobs as the guards secured her to the post at the temple entrance. "I was only admiring the flowers. They were so beautiful that I wanted to look at them more closely and smell their fragrance. As I drew the branch down, it broke off in my hand."

Tu Thuc turned to the guards. "The girl is telling the truth; I'm sure of it. Let her go. It was only an accident."

"Accident or not, she shall not go until she has paid for the damage."

"You can't leave her tied up like that," Tu Thuc protested, "exposed to the night air and the mosquitoes — or any animal that might come to attack her."

"Heaven will protect her if she is innocent." The guard cast her a contemptuous glance. "Whatever you say, she stays here until someone comes for her and pays us what she owes us for her crime — or her carelessness."

Silent in her despair, the girl slumped against the post. Her long hair, black as a raven's wing, had fallen over the tear-stained cheeks that glistened in the moonlight like ripe apricots. His heart heavy with pity, Tu Thuc glanced from one guard to the other, their faces granitelike in their determination. To say anything further in the girl's defense would be as useless as appealing to the stone gods that guarded the temple entrance.

He slipped his arms out of his brocade coat and held it out to them. "Here. Take my coat as payment for the damage," he said, "and let the girl go."

They stared at him for a moment as if in disbelief till finally one of them reached for the coat, then bent to cut the girl's bonds. Now she was free, and she was thanking him, but he scarcely heard her words. Standing there in the moonlight, she could have been one of the flowers in human form — a lily perhaps or a lotus blossom. Then suddenly she was gone; he, too, turned, as if in a trance, and made his way out of the garden and toward his home.

All night long he lay, hardly knowing whether he was asleep or awake. When he closed his eyes, he was in the garden again, and the beautiful girl was standing before him; when he opened them, she was walking away from him into the moonlight. At last the morning sun at his window drew him from his bed, but still he moved as if in a dream. Everywhere he looked, the face of the girl rose before him, and when he tried to write reports of the district's affairs, he found himself composing verses in praise of her loveliness instead. One thought constantly tormented him: Why had he not asked her her name or where she lived?

One day he could stand it no longer. Time alone seemed to bring no relief, but perhaps a change of scenery would cure him of the melancholy that haunted him. He took up a brush and wrote out his resignation.

The next morning he set off carrying nothing but a gourd of wine, his guitar and a case containing his writing implements. He had no destination in mind. Through field and forest he wandered, across streams and over mountains, along lakes and rivers, stopping whenever the beauty around him inspired him to sing a song or compose a verse.

At last he reached the sea and hired a boat to take him along the coast. He watched the shore gliding by — sandy beaches interspersed with overhanging cliffs and forests. He gazed at the ocean, as each wave chased the one before it in its mad dash to the shore. The sky gleamed blue with white puffs of clouds. He watched them change from one fantastic shape to another.

One huge cloud seemed to almost touch the horizon. The sunlight, reflected through it onto the sea, gave the cloud a rainbowlike iridescence as it formed itself into a giant cluster of water lilies resting on the surface of the water. Fascinated, Tu Thuc asked the boatman to row closer.

As they drew nearer, Tu Thuc saw the cloud was an island. Mountains of indescribable loveliness rose before him. Tu Thuc paid the boatman and sent him on his way. As if in a trance he started toward the mountains. But, alas, they greeted him like a wall of stone — impassable, impenetrable.

He stared up at the towering cliffs, shaking his head in disappointment. "What beauty must lie on the other side," he lamented. "But only with the wings of a bird could I hope to cross them." He ran his hand across the rocky surface, resigned yet reluctant to leave.

His fingers brushed a cleft in the rock, and suddenly before his eyes it began to widen. He watched in awe as a doorway opened in the side of the mountain. He ventured inside, both hands pressed to the moss-covered wall as he felt his way deeper and deeper into the cavern. The darkness pressed against him like a shroud, and he was half-tempted to turn back; yet some strange power seemed to draw him onward. Then he turned a sharp corner and found himself standing once more in the sunlight.

But it was a sunlight brighter than he had ever known before, and it dazzled him. As his eyes adjusted he saw that he was in a garden lovelier than any he had ever seen or imagined, filled with flowers of every color of the rainbow. They shone like jewels, and their individual fragrances blended into a perfume that put to shame any he had previously encountered. Before him lay a palace, its walls carved from one giant pearl which gleamed violet, then azure, emerald, and roseate in turn, as the sun's rays sported over its surface. He walked toward it as if drawn by some irresistible force.

A door opened, and two girls dressed in blue smiled at him in greeting. They glanced at each other, and their laughter tinkled like bells as one said to the other, "The bridegroom has come."

He stood as one under a spell as they walked toward him. "Our lady awaits you," they said as they led him inside.

He followed them down halls hung with brocade tapestries to a crimson door over which a motto was emblazoned in gilt letters:

Outside is illusion;
Only within is found truth.

He gazed through the open doorway. At the far end of the room, on a throne resplendent with every imaginable jewel, sat a woman robed in white. As he hesitated on the threshold, she beckoned him inside and motioned him to a seat next to her.

"You look somewhat bewildered," she said, smiling at him kindly. "No doubt all this display leaves you dazzled." She shifted her position, leaning toward him slightly. "Tell me, do you have any idea where you are?"

"My lady," Tu Thuc answered respectfully, "in all my travels I have never encountered a land to compare with this one, nor have I heard any tale of such splendors. Unless you are pleased to enlighten me, I must remain ignorant of my whereabouts."

The woman laughed as if pleased with his answer. "Of course, how would you know? Let me tell you then. You are in grotto number six of the thirty-six grottos of Fairyland. Surrounded on all sides by the sea, our land does not touch the water's surface but hovers just above the waves, appearing and disappearing from view as it is driven about by the winds and the clouds. I am the Lady Nguy, fairy queen of Mount Nam Nhac. Only because I have heard of your virtue and kindness have I invited you here to our land." She turned then to one of the girls dressed in blue, who stepped to a door behind the throne and opened it.

A girl dressed in fairy robes like rose petals stood before him, her eyes shining like diamonds and her face pink with blushes under her golden headdress—a bridal headdress. Tu Thuc felt himself almost ready to swoon with joy as he recognized the girl he had met in the garden.

Lady Nguy was speaking again. "This is my daughter, Giang Huong. Since the day that you came to her rescue, she has not been able to forget you. Now it is my wish to reward your kindness by making you my son-in-law." She clapped her hands to call all the assembled fairies to attention. "The wedding will begin at once."

Dizzy with joy, scarcely daring to hope that it was not all a dream, Tu Thuc took his place beside Giang Huong. The festivities began. Music such as he had never heard before, so exquisite that he vowed never to touch his guitar again, filled the hall. Lovely fairy children flitted here and there with goblets of sparkling, aromatic wines and platters laden with all manner of indescribable delicacies, inviting the guests to drink and to eat their fill. Tu Thuc sampled each item at their insistence. All through the day and the evening they feasted, yet Tu Thuc was never sated but felt only a sense of well-being such as he had never experienced before.

The days that followed were ones of unspeakable joy for Tu Thuc. Week followed week and month followed month as, with Giang Huong

The clouds parted momentarily, and he glimpsed the shore in the distance.

Mây tan ra cho chàng thấy bờ biển tử đằng xa.

beside him, all his wildest dreams came true. Each hour followed the one before it like a rosary of never-ending delights as they enjoyed together the beauties of the garden, the splendors of the palace, and the joy of each other's companionship.

Then one day as they strolled near the edge of the garden Tu Thuc happened to glance seaward. The clouds parted momentarily, and he glimpsed the shore in the distance. A small boat, like the one he had traveled in, bobbed up and down on the waves. Suddenly he saw himself once more in the boat, and his imagination carried him back over the sea, across the mountains and rivers to the village he had left behind. Before his eyes rose the image of his home: his parents, his brothers, and his sisters in the doorway as they had been on the morning he bade them farewell. Pain and a feeling of remorse gripped him. How were they now? Were they well? Were they wondering why he had been gone so long without sending back any word? It had been a year since he had left them.

"My love, what is it?" Giang Huong was gazing at him in concern, and she reached up to blot a tear that had escaped down his cheek.

He pointed to the boat that lay across the water. "It made me think of my home and my parents," he told her. "When I left them I had not thought to be gone so long. How could I have forgotten them so completely?"

She turned from him, sadness in her eyes. "I thought you were happy here, my love. I did not imagine your heart was still bound to the illusions of the world below."

"I am happy, and I love you with all my heart." He grasped her hands and gazed down at her, struggling to find the right words to make her understand. "All I want is to see them once more — to visit them for a few days and make sure they're all right. Then I'll come back to you and never leave you again for the rest of my life."

Her eyes sought the ground as she answered him. "Life on earth is so short that, once you return to the world below, it will not be so easy to find our land again. But I cannot ask you to stay against your will. I will ask my mother to have a carriage made ready for you."

The two of them brushed the tears from their eyes as Tu Thuc stepped into the cloud carriage. Giang Huong pressed a roll of paper into his hand. "Promise me that when you read the letter you won't forget me," she said.

He clasped her hands in farewell. "I will never forget you. In only a few days I will be back here again with you."

The carriage rose into the air, and then suddenly — before he could blink his eyes — it was descending again at the side of the road that led to his village.

But as he walked he looked around him in consternation. Everything seemed changed. The huge banyan tree that had stood at the edge of the village was no longer there, and the wooden bridge across the stream had been replaced with one of stone. Only the moss–covered rocks that lined the banks seemed familiar. As he walked into town, not one house or building that he remembered still stood in its accustomed place. In the crowds that jostled past him in the marketplace there was not a single person that he recognized, and even the clothes the people wore were strange. At last he stopped some boys playing along the road and asked them the way to his home.

"Tu Thuc?" One of the older boys repeated the name questioningly, then shook his head. "I've never heard of him."

"You must have heard of him. He was district chief until last year. This is the village of Tien Du, isn't it?"

"Yes, this is Tien Du, but our district chief is named Tran Ngoc. We've never heard of a Tu Thuc."

His head swimming in confusion, Tu Thuc pushed his way on through the crowd, stopping first one person and then another to ask for news of his family. But always the answer was the same. None of them had heard of anyone by the name of Tu Thuc.

At last he found his way to the district chief's

office. But this building, too, was changed. Only the sign over the doorway identified it for him.

The man behind the desk seemed as perplexed by his questions as had the others. He drew down a large volume from the shelf behind him and opened it, his frown deepening as he flipped back through the pages and ran his finger down the entries on each one. At last he looked up, his eyes puzzled.

"Yes, there was a Tu Thuc who was chief of this district," he told him, the words coming slowly. "But that was more than three hundred years ago during the reign of Quang Thai of the previous dynasty. According to what's recorded here, he resigned his position suddenly one day, left the village, and was never heard from again." He closed the book. "It couldn't be the party you're looking for, of course. But it's the only Tu Thuc who was ever chief of this district."

Tu Thuc stumbled out of the building, blinking at the sunlight in dismay. Through his befuddled senses the truth slowly seeped through to his consciousness. During the more than three hundred days he had spent in Fairyland, more than three hundred years had passed in the world below. How could he have imagined that a day in the fairy world was equal to an entire year among humans? He must find the cloud carriage and get back to Fairyland immediately. But the carriage was gone. It had changed into two phoenixes that flew off into the air as he stepped out of it. In his hurry to reach his home, he had scarcely noticed it at the time.

His hand squeezed over something he was holding. Giang Huong's letter. Eagerly he broke the seal and unrolled it. The message was brief, and he read it through his tears: "How can one find the fairy mountain in the vast ocean? How hard it will be for the two of us to meet again!"

He remembered the Lady Nguy's words on their wedding day: "Surrounded on all sides by the sea our land does not touch the water's surface but hovers just above the waves, appearing and disappearing from view as it is driven about by the winds and the clouds." He had found it once, only because he had happened to glance up at just the right moment as the clouds formed the lotus cluster on the horizon. Could he hope to be so fortunate again? Giang Huong had spoken correctly: In the short life allotted to humans, one could scarcely hope to find the land of the fairies once, let alone a second time.

Then her parting words came back to him: "Promise me that when you read the letter you won't forget me."

He rose to his feet. Pulling his coat around him, he picked up his walking stick and walked down the road that led away from the village toward the mountains. He would spend the rest of his life searching — searching for the land of his dreams. Someday, he knew, he would find the lotus cloud again, and when the mountain parted, Giang Huong would be standing there, her arms outstretched, waiting for him.

Master Frog

GIANG DUNG WAS A plain girl, so plain in fact that all the townspeople marveled when her parents finally found her a husband. Then they nodded their heads knowingly and whispered to one another that the young man must have been after her father's money. He had plenty of it, it was true, and Giang Dung was his only child. The day of the wedding came and passed, and the people found more interesting things to gossip about until a few months later when Giang Dung's husband died.

"It's fortunate that she's expecting a child," one person said, and the rest agreed. "At least she'll have someone to look after her in her old age. It's certain she'll never find anyone else to marry her."

But when the child was born, instead of being a boy to carry on her husband's name or at least a girl to give her some comfort and companionship, it was only a frog. And the people's tongues wagged again until they tired of the subject. "What would you expect? Giang Dung almost looks like a frog herself, she's so ugly."

Poor Giang Dung cried for days until she had no tears left. Then she resigned herself to her fate and determined to raise the frog as well as she could. If she was being punished for some unknown evil she had committed, she would have to make the best of it and serve her sentence. But on the other hand, Heaven sometimes worked in mysterious ways, and it was just possible that some great destiny lay ahead for her son.

But as the years passed, Giang Dung forgot both of these theories. Except for his strange appearance, Master Frog was really quite an ordinary boy — now mischievous, now helpful, but always affectionate. He followed her around the house as she went about her daily tasks, helping her to care for the silk worms. He gathered mulberry leaves for her to chop and place in their trays;

he watched them as they began to spin their cocoons, fascinated at the way they swung their heads down and around and then up again to surround themselves with the fine strands. He often perched beside her as she sat at the loom and thought it great fun to take the shuttle in his mouth and wriggle his small body in and out among the warp threads. Sometimes, as she was cooking, he would hop up on the stove to stir the soup, or if he was sure she was not watching him, to snap up some tasty tidbit with his long, sticky tongue. But, like other children, he was often bored with being indoors and went out to play hide-and-seek and hopscotch with the boys of the neighborhood. All in all, he was both a good-natured and an intelligent little fellow, and his mother decided at last that something must be done about his education.

"A frog? In my class?" the teacher demanded when Giang Dung brought him to the school. "Impossible! I would be the laughingstock of the town."

"Then at least let him sit at the back and listen," she pleaded with him. "I promise you he won't cause you any trouble."

As the weeks went by, Master Frog proved himself such a model student that at last the teacher

Master Frog proved himself such a model student . . .

Chàng Nhái tỏ ra mình là một học-trò rất gương-mẫu . . .

moved him up to the head of the class and often admonished the others to follow his example. At first he had tried to grasp the brush with his front feet, but later found that he could form more graceful characters if he held it in his mouth. Generally he was the first to commit a passage to memory, and if none of the others could correctly interpret a line of the reading, the teacher would call on Master Frog. Finally, Master Frog completed his education and grew to young froghood.

"It's time to think of learning some trade," Giang Dung suggested to him one day. "Tomorrow I will go to town and talk to some of the craftsmen. Perhaps one of them would be willing to take you on as an apprentice."

But Master Frog shook his head. "Mother, first I would like to get married."

"G...get married!" she stammered, almost unable to believe her ears. "I...is there any particular girl you have in mind?"

"Yes, Mother. Princess Kien Tien, the king's youngest daughter."

Giang Dung drew back in alarm. "Son, you must be out of your mind! How could you ever hope to marry the king's daughter?"

"Nevertheless I shall marry her." Master Frog planted all four feet on the table in a stance of determination. "Tomorrow I shall go to the king to ask for her hand."

All Giang Dung's protests — all her entreaties — were in vain. Master Frog had made up his mind, and nothing could change it. And so the next morning he and Giang Dung set off for the palace.

Giang Dung set him down as they entered the audience hall, and he hopped straight up to the king, bowing respectfully as he neared the throne. The king stared at him in astonishment as he made his request and then burst out laughing.

"So you want to marry my daughter," he said. "Well, I have three daughters. Which one is it you want? But don't be in a hurry to make up your mind." His lips twisted in amusement as he motioned to one of the courtiers. "Bring Their Royal Highnesses here."

"Come here, my dears," he beckoned to them as they entered the hall. "A suitor has presented himself to request the hand of one of you." With a grand sweep of his forearm he indicated Master Frog at the foot of the throne. "He has not yet told me the extent of his kingdom or the number of vassals who pay him tribute, but does he not have a noble air?" He turned back to Master Frog. "Allow me to introduce my daughters to Your Highness: Kim Chau," he pointed to the first, who cast a contemptuous glance in Master Frog's direction, then gave her head such a violent toss that one of her pearl hairpins slipped from its place and fell to the floor; "Bich Ngoc," he indicated the second, who made a face at him and stuck out her tongue, "and Kien Tien," he presented the last of the three, who had stood the whole time, her hands folded in her long sleeves and her eyes on the floor. "Now would you please tell me which of the three pleases you?"

Kim Chau's chin rose a trifle higher. "I won't marry him, Father."

"I'll kill myself if you force me to marry him," Bich Ngoc declared with a stamp of her foot.

"Your Majesty," Master Frog interrupted them, "it is Kien Tien whose hand I have come to seek."

"Enough of this charade." The king's face had grown angry. "We have carried this joke far enough." He motioned to the guards. "Take this presumptuous creature out of my sight at once and execute him."

As the king finished speaking, Master Frog croaked in a loud voice. Suddenly the building began to shake as lightning flashed and thunder roared. On all sides the doors flew open, and the guards cowered in terror as wild beasts of every description burst into the hall. Elephants trumpeted as they stampeded in, tigers roared, leopards and panthers growled as they sprang from one corner to another.

"A few minutes ago Your Majesty inquired about my vassals," Master Frog's croak rose above the uproar. "They have come. I will leave them here to answer any questions you may have about the extent of my kingdom. Until we meet again, Your Majesty." Master Frog turned and hopped toward the exit.

"Wait! Wait!" the king shouted after him as a tiger leapt over his throne pursuing a panther in a game of tag. "You can't leave us like this, surrounded by all these wild beasts." But Master Frog only hopped over their backs, one after another, as he made his way to the door. "Daughters, what shall we do?"

"I wouldn't marry a frog if he were the son of Jade Emperor!" Kim Chau's voice was as haughty as ever, though she winced as a leopard brushed past her.

Bich Ngoc covered her face as a bear lumbered toward her. "I'd rather be torn limb from limb!" she screeched.

"Father, I'll marry him." Kien Tien squeezed between two elephants to the king's side. "It's not right for us to think only of ourselves when the whole kingdom may be in danger. And the frog cannot be such a bad sort. He's obviously an individual of great power, yet he does not appear to be cruel. With all these beasts surrounding us, not one of us has been harmed."

As she finished speaking the uproar ceased, and one by one the beasts filed from the hall. Master Frog stood alone before the king.

"I will send the engagement gifts tomorrow," he said as he, too, turned and hopped from the room.

A few days later the wedding was celebrated with great pomp and ceremony. Kings and dignitaries of all the surrounding countries came to pay their respects, and no one dared to laugh at Master Frog or the princess, for the tales of his great power had spread far and wide.

During the weeks that followed, Master Frog and Kien Tien lived together happily as the two came to understand each other better and to care for each other more deeply. In spite of his ugliness, Kien Tien found him such an intelligent and such a pleasant companion that, as the days went by, she grew genuinely fond of him. Then one morning she awoke to find the frog lying dead on the pillow beside her.

With a cry she lifted her husband's body to her lips, kissing it again and again as her tears wet the mottled green skin. Someone called her name, and she looked up to see a handsome young man standing next to the bed, his arms outstretched as if to embrace her.

She backed away from him, crying out in alarm. "How dare you come here?" she demanded. "Can't you see my husband is dead and I am mourning him?" Suddenly her eyes narrowed. "Or was it you who killed him, you miserable creature!" She burst into fresh tears. "You shall surely die for your crime!"

The man smiled. "No, Kien Tien. I am Master Frog. What you are holding there is only my skin, which I shed during the night." He sat down beside her. "I am a fairy, a heavenly mandarin, one of the sons of Jade Emperor. I was bored with the life in Fairyland and wanted to seek adventure in the world below. But when I asked my father's permission, he was angry with me. He said he would grant my request but that I must be born as a frog. Only if I could succeed in that form would I be able to resume my true shape. Now I have proved myself and am allowed to shed the frog's skin. But you must put the skin away carefully where no harm can come to it because, if it should ever be destroyed, I would have to return immediately to Jade Emperor's palace."

Overjoyed at her good fortune, Kien Tien did as he said. The days that followed were full of joy for the newlyweds. The king was filled with pride at the handsomeness and intelligence of his son-in-law, which matched so well the beauty and talent of his youngest daughter. He took them wherever he went to show them off. On every trip that he made to the surrounding countries, they accompanied him in his golden palanquin, and when he rode through the streets of the capital, they sat beside him on the back of his white elephant, cheered by all who watched them pass.

"Why didn't he tell us who he was in the first place?" Kim Chau grumbled to her sister as they watched the parade from the palace balcony. "Was it fair to come in that ugly old frog skin and then change into a handsome prince after he'd married Kien Tien?"

"If she was dumb enough to marry a frog, he should have stayed a frog," Bich Ngoc grunted in agreement.

"He should be punished for his deception. What right did he have to ask for Kien Tien anyway? I'm the oldest."

"Kien Tien says he's a son of Jade Emperor,

but I don't believe it. He's probably nothing but an ordinary frog. Why don't we see if we can find his skin and have a look at it?"

The sisters went to Kien Tien's room, searching through chest after chest and shelf after shelf till at last, among a pile of her most precious silks, they found what they were looking for.

"She hid it well enough," Kim Chau sniffed. "No wonder. It's an ugly old thing, isn't it?"

Bich Ngoc reached for it, turning it over in her hands. "It certainly is. And just as I thought, nothing but an ordinary frog skin." She squinted her eyes thoughtfully. "Who knows but what, if we caught a couple of frogs for ourselves, they might shed their skins for us? There might be a handsome prince in any one of them if we could just get him to come out." She stuffed Master Frog's skin into her sash as the two of them hurried out to the pond.

Day by day Kim Chau and Bich Ngoc watched their chosen frogs, waiting for the hoped-for transformation. They fed them on the most delicious foods; petted them; cooed endearments and whispered promises of fame, fortune, and riches in their ears. And each night they gently laid them on the pillow next to them, certain that the coming morning would bring the answer to their dreams. But nothing happened; both frogs remained as they were when they had fished them from the pond.

"There has to be a prince in there!" Bich Ngoc cried one morning in exasperation. "And I'm not going to wait any longer to find him." She picked up a knife and began to skin the poor creature alive.

Kim Chau snatched up her own frog and followed her example. But before they were finished it was plain that no prince was to be found. In disgust the sisters threw the corpses into the fireplace.

Bich Ngoc jerked Master Frog's skin from her belt. "I don't know what I'm still carrying this around for," she grunted as she tossed it into the fire.

Meanwhile in Kien Tien's room, she and Master Frog were just getting out of bed. Suddenly he gave a cry of pain.

"My chest, my arms, my legs are burning!" he cried. "My whole body is on fire."

As Kien Tien rushed to his side, he fell to the floor, writhing in agony. Moments later he lay lifeless in her arms. Kien Tien pressed him close to her, weeping bitterly.

"It must be because you burned his old frog skin," Kim Chau whispered to Bich Ngoc when they heard what had happened. "What are we going to do? Sooner or later she'll discover the skin is missing, and if she finds out we took it and tells Father ..."

Bich Ngoc clapped her hand over her sister's mouth. "We aren't going to sit around and wait for that to happen!"

Together they went to Kien Tien's room, where she lay on the bed weeping. They sat down beside her, stroking her hair to comfort her.

"Come, little sister, it's a terrible tragedy, but you mustn't spend the whole day lying here crying." Bich Ngoc poured some tea from the teapot on the table, dropping a little sleeping powder into the cup as she carried it back to the bed. "Here, drink something warm. It'll make you feel better."

Kien Tien raised her head, sipping the hot liquid as Bich Ngoc held it to her lips. Then she lay down again and was soon fast asleep.

Quickly the sisters lifted her and carried her outside to the carriage. As fast as they could make the horses go they rode out of town to the seaside. Then, making sure that no one was around, they shoved their sister out of the carriage, watching with satisfaction as she hit the surface of the water and sank beneath the waves. Then they rushed home to tell their father that Kien Tien had committed suicide.

"We tried to stop her," Bich Ngoc sobbed into her handkerchief. "But she wouldn't listen to us. She was so miserable at the thought of never seeing Master Frog again that she threw herself into the sea. The waves carried her away before we could call for help."

Suddenly gasps rose throughout the audience hall. Master Frog had entered the room.

He approached the throne, bowing respectfully. "Jade Emperor has allowed me to return to the earth to complete my lifetime," he told the king. "But why is everyone crying? What has happened?" He gazed from one person to another, seeking an answer.

"Dear brother-in-law, our sister is dead." Bich Ngoc wiped the tears from her eyes as she spoke. "She was so overcome with sorrow at losing you that she threw herself into the sea." She stepped closer to him, laying her hand on his arm. "I know what a shock it is for you. But Kim Chau and I will do everything we can to help. Either one of us would be willing to take our sister's place."

But Master Frog was already running toward the door. At his order a horse was saddled, and he leapt on its back, riding at top speed toward the sea. Fearlessly he dove in, letting his body sink to the bottom. Swiftly he ran across the ocean floor to the Crystal Palace and, bursting through the gates, prostrated himself before the Dragon King of the Waters.

The Dragon King gazed down at him kindly. "Stand up, nephew. What you are seeking may be behind you."

As Master Frog rose, a company of shrimps and turtles entered the hall. One of them bore Kien Tien in his arms.

"My soldiers have found your wife," the Dragon King told him. "I would have let her live here in my palace, but since you've come for her, you may take her home with you."

Master Frog rushed toward her joyfully. As he lifted her from the turtle-soldier's arms, she opened her eyes and smiled up at him. Then both of them fell at the Dragon King's feet to thank him for his mercy.

Master Frog led Kien Tien out of the Crystal Palace and up through the water to the shore,

"My soldiers have found your wife," the Dragon King told him.

Hải-Long Vương phán rằng: "Binh tướng của trẫm đã tìm được vợ của con rồi."

where his horse was waiting. Together they rode back to the palace.

Kim Chau glanced down from her balcony to see Master Frog reining his horse below. She drew back in alarm and called to her sister.

"We're done for," she trembled, grabbing Bich Ngoc's arm and pulling her after her. "Kien Tien will tell Father everything."

The two of them raced down the stairs and out a back way. "We'll hide in the forest," Bich Ngoc decided. "No one will find us there."

And the two were never seen or heard of again. But as for Kien Tien and Master Frog, they lived happily ever after, loved and respected by all for their kind deeds. Before many days had passed, they had Giang Dung brought to the palace, where she lived in comfort and happiness to a ripe old age. In due time Master Frog became king and, with Kien Tien as his queen, ruled their people in peace and prosperity for many long years.

The Lampstand Princess

⟢⟤⟣⟢

IN OLDEN TIMES AT THE court of the capital of Vietnam, there reigned a king who had only one child, a daughter named Quynh Dao, whom he loved more than anything else in the world. Many were the suitors who had come seeking her hand, for the fame of her beauty had spread even to the neighboring countries; but the king rejected them all, preferring to keep his daughter at his side. Then one day an embassy arrived from the court of China led by Prince Hoang Truu, the emperor's son. Hoang Truu, too, had heard tales of Quynh Dao's beauty, and after one glimpse of her, he knew that he must have her as his bride.

"I will go home and secure my father's permission," he told the king, who had at last given his consent. For how could he refuse the son of the Emperor of China? "Then I will send ships laden with wedding gifts to bring Quynh Dao to China."

At last the day came that Quynh Dao sighted the approaching ships from her lookout at the highest tower of the palace. For weeks she had watched the horizon, straining her eyes for the first glimpse of the dragon figureheads that would take her to China and to the side of the handsome prince who had pleaded so eloquently for her hand.

The days that followed were filled with excitement as the imperial matchmakers presented the gifts and received the king's formal acceptance. Feast followed banquet until, at last, Quynh Dao, half tearful, half fluttery with anticipation, embraced her father one last time and boarded the ship for her journey.

Quynh Dao leaned against the railing, watching the waves lap the side of the ship as it sped along. The sun shone down warm, sparkling on the water's surface. Above, the sky was blue with scarcely a cloud, except for a few that were just beginning to darken the northeastern sky. As they inched along toward the sun, sky and water dulled to a dirty gray. Without warning the rain began, striking the deck in torrents. Quynh Dao and her maids turned to seek cover, grasping at each other for support as the ship rocked to and fro.

Sailors were running back and forth across the deck, adjusting the sails, trying to steer out of the storm. The oarsmen rowed furiously; but they were no match for the wind, which had caught the ship like a toy in the hands of an angry giant, tossing it from one side to the other. Quynh Dao heard the sound of boards splintering, then the swish of water rushing in through the cracks. The ship pitched violently to one side, throwing her to the deck with the others, tearing each from the arms of her companions. Clutching desperately at the air, she felt herself sliding across the deck. Frantically she grasped the railing, feeling it give way as a wave leaped over the side and lifted her struggling body in its embrace. The railing was still in her hands; she clung to it as the waves washed over her, drowning her cries and the shouts of her

The sun beating down on her face at last awoke her.

Ánh nắng mặt trời đánh thức nàng dậy.

maids. She felt the darkness enveloping her. She was slipping away, away, sliding into some bottomless cavern. Then she knew nothing more.

The sun beating down on her face at last awoke her. Quynh Dao opened her eyes and looked around her. She was lying on a beach, the ship's railing still clutched in her hands. Slowly she pulled herself to her feet, brushing the sand from her clothes. As far as she could see, the sea stretched before her, but only a gull here and there disturbed the roll of the waves. No ship was in sight. On either side of her, sand dunes rose, then dipped toward the horizon, and behind her the clumps of trees that dotted the beach gradually thickened into dense forest.

Where was she, and how far ahead of her lay the Chinese capital? She had no way of knowing, but, if she followed the coastline, she was sure to reach it eventually. If she stayed in this deserted location, she would surely starve to death. With a sigh she turned her face toward the north, the sea on her right hand and the forest on her left.

For days she trudged on, finding food and water in the berry bushes and streams of the forest, seeking refuge at night in some cave or grotto. Sometimes she met a kindly fisherman or woodcutter who gave her a bowl of rice, with what fish and vegetables he and his family could spare, and a mat and a pillow for the night. But always the next morning she was on her way again until, at last, one day she could make out the walls of the city in the distance.

Feeling renewed strength at the sight, she rushed toward them and found her way to the palace. But the guards laughed at her, then ordered her rudely to move on.

"You want to see His Highness, the Prince of the Eastern Palace? What business could the likes of you have with him? Go back to your fields and buffaloes where you belong."

Quynh Dao looked down at her torn, soiled garments and felt the tears come to her eyes. But she blinked them back furiously. It would do no good to tell them that she was the Vietnamese princess, the bride their master was waiting for. At best they would only laugh at her; at worst they might throw her into prison for her presumption. She must find another way to enter the palace and find the prince for herself.

"But, sirs, there must be something even I can do," she begged. "Please don't turn me away after I have walked so far and spent all my money on the journey."

"Well, if you wanted work, why didn't you say so in the first place?" One of the guards turned back to her with a grunt. "It seems someone mentioned that Her Royal Highness, Princess Huy, was looking for a nursemaid for her child." He examined Quynh Dao doubtfully. "You're awfully dirty, but maybe if you washed up a bit she might take you. Come with me, and I'll see what I can do for you."

Princess Huy was lounging in a lacquered armchair when Quynh Dao entered the room some time later. Quynh Dao stood just inside the door waiting while the maids finished plaiting their lady's hair and painting her fingernails. She would have to wait for the right moment to tell her who she was, Quynh Dao mused as she watched her through respectfully lowered eyelids — unless she could manage to find Hoang Truu first.

Princess Huy straightened up in the chair and took the mirror that the maid was holding out to her. Turning it this way and that, she tilted her head first to one side and then to the other, squinting her eyes at the elaborate tower of ebony that crowned her head. She patted here and there at an invisible flaw before she sighed her acceptance.

"It'll do; it'll do, I suppose," she muttered as she returned the mirror. She turned at last to Quynh Dao, still waiting by the door. "Yes, yes." Her voice was brisk and impatient. "Who are you, and what do you want?"

"May it please Your Royal Highness, I was told that you were looking for a nursemaid." Quynh Dao curled her toes into the carpet to keep her knees from shaking. "I would like to apply for the position."

"You're rather young, and I don't imagine you've had much experience with children." She examined her critically, hesitating for a long moment. "But I suppose I might as well give you a try." She clapped her hands, and one of the maids rose to her feet. "See if Hong Hoa has awakened from her nap and bring her here to me."

The maid scurried from the room and returned a few minutes later, leading a small girl of two or three by the hand. Princess Huy beckoned to her, and the child inched up to her, her chubby fingers clutching at the string of pearls around her neck.

Princess Huy put an arm around her shoulders to draw her closer and extended her other hand toward Quynh Dao. "Mother's found a new nurse for you, my dear," she said to the child. "Do you think you will like her?"

Their eyes met, and Quynh Dao reached out to enfold the child's small hands between both of hers. Hong Hoa's face broke into a grin.

"Yes, Mother, I like her," she replied. "Please let her stay here with me."

Princess Huy turned to Quynh Dao. "Hong Hoa likes to play outside in the garden after her nap. Let her sail her boat in the lotus pond," she added, as the child took the toy from one of the maids. "But make sure she doesn't fall in the water."

Stifling a sigh of relief, Quynh Dao led her toward the door. The garden bloomed with flowers of all colors, many of which she had never seen before. A few steps ahead she saw the lotus pond, its surface dotted with green pads from which rose clumps of pink and white flowers. A flock of geese completed the scene, some skimming between the lily pads while others waddled along the water's edge.

Hong Hoa tugged at Quynh Dao's hand, drawing her toward the little pier at the edge of the pond. She kicked off her tiny slippers and stuck her toes into the cool water, laughing merrily as she splashed at a goose paddling by. Then, tiring of the game, Hong Hoa drew up her legs, squatted over the edge of the pier, and dropped her boat into the water, guiding it among the lily pads with a long stick. The string of pearls left the child's chest and hovered precariously about her chin. Quynh Dao slipped it off and hung it carefully from the branch of an overhanging tree.

The afternoon passed swiftly in the pleasant garden, and soon it was time for Hong Hoa to go in. Quynh Dao dried her feet and helped her into her slippers. Then she reached for the pearls. But only the leaves met her gaze. She ran her eyes up and down the branch, unable to believe what she saw. The pearls were gone! It was impossible! No one else had been in the garden. No one could have taken the pearls.

Frantically she scanned the branch again, then the ground under it. She had hung them there; she was sure of it. If they had slipped and fallen, they could not be far away. She crawled up and down the garden, examining each inch of the land, looking under every tree and running her hands over every flower. She turned out Hong Hoa's pockets and her own, again and again. But it was useless. The necklace had vanished.

Finally there was nothing left to do but go in and report the incident to Princess Huy.

Huy's face grew red with anger as she listened to her story. "You've taken the necklace and hidden it somewhere," she shouted. "But don't think you will get away with it. I'll beat the truth out of you if I have to break every rod in the country to do it." She stepped to the brass gong that hung on the wall and struck it until it shook with the impact. "Take this good-for-nothing wretch outside and tie her up," she ordered the servants who hurried to answer the summons, "and bring me a whip."

Not until the back of Quynh Dao's blouse was stained with blood did Huy cast aside her whip.

"Untie her now," she said to the servants. She glanced down at Quynh Dao's limp form contemptuously. "You still won't tell me where you've hidden the pearls? Very well then. Maybe I know a way to soften your hard head." She grasped her by one arm, jerking her to her feet. "Get back inside and I'll show you what your job will be from now on."

Pushing her into the room, she stepped to the table and picked up the oil lamp, shoving it into Quynh Dao's hands. "Put it on your head. From now on you will be my lampstand." She drew the lacquered chair over to her dressing table and opened her jewel chest. "Come stand over here so I can see what I'm doing."

Biting her lips to keep back the tears, Quynh Dao did as she commanded. With each breath, her blouse rubbed against her raw back. Already her arms ached from holding the lamp, and the hot metal burned her forehead. Rivulets of sweat dampened her hair and streamed down her face. Her whole body cried out for relief; but still she

Quynh Dao stood as usual, holding the lamp on her head . . .

Quỳnh Dao đứng đội đèn như mọi hôm . . .

stood, stiffly at attention, until at last Princess Huy gave the order to put out the lamp and went to bed.

One evening Quynh Dao stood, as usual, holding the lamp on her head, as Huy dealt the cards around her circle of friends. She sighed inwardly as each player laid a stack of coins on the table. It was sure to be another long night.

A knock sounded on the door, and moments later Huy called out as it opened, "Little Brother! You're just in time to join our game." She beckoned to one of the maids to pull up another chair. "Come sit over here next to me. We'll deal you in."

Quynh Dao felt her heart quicken with excitement as Hoang Truu came around the table. He stopped suddenly, his hand on the back of the chair, and stared at her. Their eyes met, and Quynh Dao blinked furiously to keep the tears from overflowing.

"I see you've noticed my new lampstand. Quite a curiosity, don't you think?" Huy's laugh ended in a rasp as she told her brother the story. "Even if she hasn't given me any light on the whereabouts of the pearls, at least she brightens up the room. And the hot oil may yet melt her obstinacy." She grasped Hoang Truu's arm, giving him a little shake. "Well, what do you think of my idea? How do you like my invention?"

He started. "Oh! Quite interesting," he finally murmured. "But really, I can't tell till I try it myself. Could you let me...uh...borrow your lampstand for a few hours?"

Huy laughed. "Yes, of course. But sit down, sit down. Play a hand or two with us before you go."

Hoang Truu shook his head. "I'm feeling tired tonight. I only stopped by to say hello." He shoved the chair in toward the table. "But I'd like to take your lampstand with me if you don't mind. She can leave the lamp here. I'll use my own lamp."

Gratefully Quynh Dao lowered her arms and placed the lamp on the table, then turned to follow Hoang Truu to the door. Now she could not keep back the tears any longer. Padding down the long vermilion halls, a few steps behind the prince, she dabbed her sleeve again and again to her eyes.

At last Hoang Truu opened a door, and she stepped inside after him. He closed it carefully, then turned to her, his own eyes misty. They stood for a moment, gazing at each other in silence until finally Hoang Truu spoke.

"Quynh Dao! Is it really you?" He reached for her hands as the tears ran down her cheeks. "When I heard your ship had sunk with everyone on board, I gave up all hope of ever seeing you again."

He led her over to a divan and listened attentively as she told him the whole story. His eyes flashed with indignation as she reached the part about the lost necklace.

"You say you hung it on a branch in my sister's garden?"

"Yes, by the pier. Next to the lotus pond."

"Ah, yes. Where she keeps her geese." His chin was sunk in his hands, and his eyes traced the pattern of the rug thoughtfully. It was a long moment before he spoke again. "I think I may know what happened. We'll find out tomorrow." He rose to his feet, drawing her up after him. "I'll have a talk with my father in the morning. But for tonight I don't want you to go back to my sister. I'll have one of the maids find you a place to sleep."

Quynh Dao sank between the silk sheets, burying her face in the soft pillow. Relief seeped into every muscle of her aching body as she drifted off to sleep. Almost before she knew it the morning sun was shining in through the draperies, spreading the new warmth in her heart throughout her body.

She opened her eyes and stared up at the maid standing next to her bed. A garment of rich blue brocade shimmered over her arm.

"His Royal Highness, the Prince of the Eastern Palace, is waiting to see you," the maid said as Quynh Dao pushed back the covers. Dressed in the finery Hoang Truu had provided for her, Quynh Dao stepped out into the hall to join him.

"I've ordered a feast to celebrate your arrival," he told her. "I'm on my way to the kitchen to see that the cooks are carrying out my instructions." He smiled at her. "I'd like you to come with me."

The head cook stepped up to them as they entered the kitchen. "We've begun the preparations," he said, "but Your Highness hasn't told us how many guests will be present or how many geese you wish us to prepare."

Hoang Truu nodded. "Prepare the geese one by one. I'll let you know when we have enough."

Hoang Truu and Quynh Dao stood to one side as the work began. One after another the geese were cleaned and quartered, then placed on the fire. Suddenly the cook gave a cry. There within the body of the goose before him lay a string of pearls.

Hoang Truu reached for the necklace. "That will be all the geese we need for the banquet," he said, "but make sure you prepare them well. You are preparing my wedding feast." He turned to Quynh Dao. "Come. My father is waiting to see you."

The emperor's face grew red with indignation as he listened to Hoang Truu's account, and he turned to one of the courtiers as soon as he finished.

"Call my daughter at once," he commanded. He adjusted the wide, jeweled belt that encircled his waist. "We shall see what kind of lesson it will take to soften her hard heart."

Princess Huy came into the room, bowing respectfully before her father. She glanced at Hoang Truu, and as her eyes shifted to Quynh Dao standing beside him, her face paled.

"Your brother has just told me what you have done," the emperor thundered. He took Quynh Dao by the hand, drawing her forward. "Do you know who this is? She's the daughter of the Vietnamese king, your brother's betrothed. We thought she had perished at sea, but Heaven preserved her and brought her to us. Only she had the misfortune to fall into your cruel hands. I've known for a long time what your true nature is, and too long I have failed to correct you. But this time you have gone too far." He turned to the guards who stood behind him. "Take her outside and whip her the way she did her sister-in-law. Then bring her back and let her be the lampstand for my son's wedding."

"No! Father, please." Quynh Dao dropped to her knees at his feet. "What she has done is past and cannot be changed. But today is a new day. Please, Father, for my sake forgive her. Don't let anything spoil the joy of your son's wedding day!"

The angry lines in the emperor's face softened as he smiled down at her. "For your sake, daughter, I will forgive her." He turned back to Huy. "Do you see the kind of person your sister is? If this does not soften your heart, nothing I could say or do would make any impression on you." He drew Quynh Dao to her feet. "Now come here and greet your sister and then help her prepare herself for the wedding festivities."

Quynh Dao reached out to grasp Huy's hands as she stepped toward her. The two gazed at each other, and Huy's eyes softened as she spoke.

"Come with me, little sister. The wedding garments that we've prepared for you are in my apartment."

Author's Notes

The Brocaded Slipper

The phoenix (*phụng* or *phượng*), the bird that graced Tấm's slippers, is one of the four mythical creatures of Vietnamese tradition, the others being the dragon, the unicorn, and the giant tortoise. The phoenix is the symbol of happiness and good fortune, and paired with the dragon, a favorite subject for Vietnamese New Year cards.

The custom of chewing betel is still seen in Việt-Nam today, though now chiefly among the older generation. A nut of the areca palm is wrapped in a leaf of the betel vine, a little quicklime is applied, and then the wad is placed in the mouth and chewed, but not swallowed. The juice, which is expectorated, is a bright blood-red. The taste is rather hot and bitter, and the effect on the chewer is somewhat stimulating and habituating. Chewing betel is a social custom and a sign of friendship between those who chew together. In olden times, offering a chew of betel to another was said to be a perfect way to strike up an acquaintance, especially with someone of the opposite sex. Today, while it is unusual to find younger people chewing betel, it is still seen at weddings, funerals, and other ceremonies.

Instead of celebrating birthdays as Americans do, the Vietnamese commemorate the death day of their relatives, especially that of their parents and grandparents. Each year on the anniversary of the ancestor's death, his or her descendants and other close relatives gather to eat a feast in the ancestor's honor. Since the ancestor's spirit is believed to rejoin the family for this occasion, a portion is set aside for him or her and placed on the ancestor's altar, a tablelike piece of furniture found in traditional Vietnamese homes. (The food does not disappear, of course, because the ancestor, being a spirit, partakes of only the smell of the food, which may afterward be removed and eaten by the family.) It is customary to have betel leaves and areca nuts at this ceremony, as well as any food of which the ancestor was especially fond during his or her lifetime.

Little Finger of the Watermelon Patch

In Vietnamese tradition dragons are the wisest and most auspicious of creatures. Not only do they bring the rainfall, but they also tour the earth during the New Year season, bringing good luck to all who are fortunate enough to be visited by them. According to Vietnamese legend, the Vietnamese themselves are descended from fifty sons of a dragon and a fairy, one of whom (Hùng Vương) became the first king of Việt-Nam. The dragon, both as a word (*long*) and as a symbol, is synonymous with wealth, prosperity, and royalty.

To the Vietnamese no meal is a real meal without rice. For a picnic lunch the rice is cooked wetter than usual, then molded into patties. While leaves were not generally used as napkins, banana leaves often served as both "Handi-Wrap" and "paper plates" in old Việt-Nam; even today various kinds of leaves are used for such purposes.

Little Finger's Vietnamese name is Nàng Út, *út* being a word that refers both to the little finger and to the youngest child. *Nàng* signifies a girl, similar to our word *Miss*. *Hậu* has the dual meaning of *kind, generous,* and *behind, in back, bringing up the rear.*

The Fairy Grotto

"Long ago during the Trần dynasty, in the reign of Quang Thái (1388–1398), there was a young man...named Tử Thức, who held the office of chief of the district of Tiên Du, which belongs to the present-day province of Bắc Ninh... "

Thus the story of Tử Thức, in spite of its fantastic circumstances, is set in a definite time in history, a definite place on the map — about twenty miles northeast of Hà-nội. The whereabouts of the fairy grotto, of course, is not so precise.

Vietnamese fairy tales are largely a legacy of Taoism, a philosophy and religion that originated more than two thousand years ago in China. In the world of Taoist Việt-Nam any animal might be a fairy in disguise; any mountain cave, any river or stream might be the abode of spirits. The fairy who involved herself (or, less often, himself) in human affairs usually did so to her sorrow. Only rarely was a mortal permitted to enter the fairy world, as Từ Thức did.

Occasionally a fairy might appear briefly to offer help to a deserving mortal, in which case she could usually be recognized by her dress — her flowing robes and especially the long sash that billowed around her and the tasseled wand that she carried. But when she wished to consort with humans as equals, she generally disguised herself in more conventional dress.

In ancient times the Vietnamese, under the influence of China, wore long robes with high collars and flowing sleeves. The traditional Vietnamese dress, however, is the *áo dài* — literally, "long *áo*," *áo* being the general word for any garment that covers the upper part of the body. Nowadays only women wear the *áo dài* — the high-collared, long-sleeved, fitted tunic slit on both sides to the waist to form a front and a back panel and worn over black or white pants. But formerly men wore a similar garment, though shorter (mid-calf length) and more loosely fitting. The usual material was silk, of which there were many types and grades. Garments of brocade, not necessarily of silk, were an indication of wealth.

Master Frog

There was no cry of "back to the basics" among the educators of old Việt-Nam. No one would have thought of teaching anything else. If one were going to get anywhere in life — that is, pass the civil service exams held once every three years and receive his appointment as mandarin (public official) — he had better commit to memory as much of the classics as he could. Rote memorization was stressed but so also was explaining the text and being able to put one's own ideas into verse. Every educated Vietnamese was a poet, and the ability to answer a poetic challenge with a verse of one's own was highly prized.

In olden times Vietnamese was written using characters adapted from the Chinese. Instead of pens, people wrote with brushes, and beautiful handwriting was considered an art and often used as decoration. Today the Vietnamese use the Roman alphabet, just as we do. This alphabet was adapted to the Vietnamese language by Alexandre de Rhodes, a French priest who went to Việt-Nam during the seventeenth century.

Jade Emperor — Ngọc Hoàng in Vietnamese — was king of the gods and fairies, the supreme deity of Taoism. He lived in a beautiful palace on the banks of the Milky Way, which the Vietnamese call the Silver River (Ngân-Hà), attended by a court of heavenly mandarins not too different from that of his human counterparts. The seas were ruled by the Dragon King (Hải Long Vương), whose home at the bottom of the sea was known as the Crystal Palace (Thủy-tinh Cung).

Master Frog is called Chàng Nhái in Vietnamese.

The Lampstand Princess

The association between China, the Greater Dragon, and Việt-Nam, the Smaller Dragon, has been a long relationship of political exploitation and cultural interchange. The Vietnamese had barely entered the period of recorded history when their kingdom was annexed by the Chinese. Not until a thousand years later, in the middle of the tenth century A.D., did the Vietnamese achieve a lasting, though not a total, independence. In exchange for recognition by the emperor of China, the Vietnamese kings paid them tribute at regular intervals.

Việt-Nam has had many names throughout its history, and its capital has been in a number of locations. Huế, the capital of the last Vietnamese dynasty (1802-1945), is famous for its grand palaces and other fine buildings. Previously the capital had long been located at Thăng Long, the modern-day Hà-nội.

The Vietnamese equivalent of *crown prince* was *Prince of the Eastern Palace* (Đông-cung Thái-tử). The palace of the king or emperor was not one building but actually a complex of many palaces, a city within a city. The eastern palace was the home of the crown prince.

The name Hồng Hoa means *rose* (literally, *pink flower*). Quỳnh Dao means *precious stones*.

Pronunciation of Vietnamese Names

Vietnamese is a tonal language, whose six tones are represented by marks placed over or under the vowels. Other marks indicate vowel sound or length. The middle tone, which carries no mark, has the pitch of an English word at the beginning of a sentence. The high tone, indicated by an acute accent (´), has the pitch of a word at the end of an English question. The low tone, indicated by a grave accent (`), has the pitch of a word at the end of an ordinary statement. The two rising tones ('and ~) start slightly below mid-level and glide upward to slightly above mid-level. The final tone, indicated by a dot under the vowel, is the most difficult of all. It starts lower than the low tone and rises slightly with a staccato effect. The various Vietnamese tones can be represented approximately by the following sentences:

You're gỏing? You áre? Oh! You're nòt.

While in English a change in pitch reflects only the emotions of the speaker, in Vietnamese it changes the meaning of the word, as seen by the following examples:

ma — ghost, má — mother, mà — but, mả — tomb, mã — horse, mạ — rice seedling.

Pronounce *ng* as in *singer; igh* as in *high; ow* as in *how;* $\overline{oo}$ as in *too; ŏŏ* as in *took.*

áo dài (ow yigh).

Bắc Ninh (bock nin).

Bích Ngọc (bit ngowp).

Cẩm (calm).

Chàng Nhái (chahng nyigh).

Đông-cung Thái-tử (dowm cōōm tie tŏŏ-ŏŏ).

Giảng Dung (yah-ahng yōōm).

Giáng Hương (yahng hŏŏ-ung).

Hải Long Vương (high-igh lowm vŏŏ-ung).

Hà-nội (ha no-ee).

Hậu (how).

Hoàng Trù'u (hwahng troo-ōō).

Hồng Hoa (howm hwah).

Huế (whey).

Hùng Vương (whom vớo–ung).

Huy (whee).

Kiển Tiên (kee–en tee–en).

Kim Châu (keem chow).

Lâm Tài (lum tie).

Nam Nhạc (nom nyock).

Nàng Út (nahng ōop).

Ngân-Hà (ngun ha).

Ngọc Hoàng (ngowp hwahng).

Ngụy (ngwee).

Phụng (fōom) or Phượng (fớo–ung).

Quang Thái (kwahng tie).

Quỳnh Dao (quinn yow).

Tấm (tum).

Thăng Long (tahng lowm).

Thủy-tinh Cung (twee-ee tin cōom).

Tiên Du (tee-en you).

Trần Ngọc (trun ngowp)

Từ Thức (tớo tớok).

Việt-Nam (vee–et nahm).

There are several spellings of the name Viet-Nam. While *Việt-Nam* is the correct spelling in Vietnamese, *Vietnam* is the form generally used in English.